dick bruna

miffy's house

World International

This is the house where Miffy lives

it is not very tall

it has some bright red shutters, and

the rooms are nice and small.

Miff has a little table

the bowl is Miffy's, too

and Miffy eats her breakfast

with her special Miffy spoon.

The cup is Miffy's own as well:

a very useful cup

it has a handle on each side

to help her drink it up.

Miffy has a row of pegs

to keep her coats all neat,

and underneath two shiny boots

to fit upon her feet.

Her toys go in a basket

where Miffy keeps them all,

not in the middle of the room

but neatly by the wall.

Her bright blue engine fits inside

so does her yellow bear,

a ball of many colours and

her other toys are there.

Miffy has her little chair

on which she likes to rest

sometimes she sits there on her own

but with her doll is best.

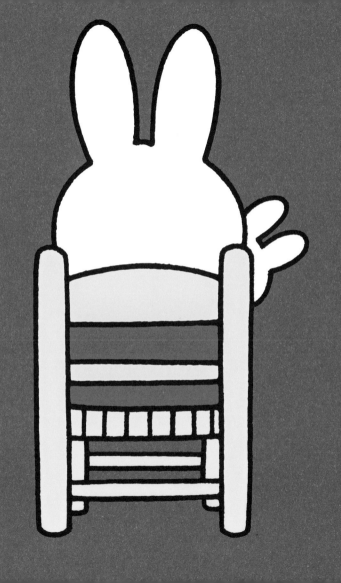

Then there's a cupboard for her clothes

that is both tall and wide,

the cupboard has red doorknobs

and lots of room inside.

Her dresses hang inside it

each on a different hook,

you see the one with flowers on –

her pretty party frock.

And then there are her dungarees

which may be new to you,

and you can see there on the front

they have a pocket too.

A clock is hanging on the wall

it goes tick-tock, tick-tock

when Miffy looks she sees the time

is nearly seven o'clock.

And when it reaches seven

then Miffy, just like you,

must go to bed, because for her

the day is over too.

miffy's library

miffy
miffy goes to stay
miffy is crying
miffy's birthday
miffy at school
miffy's bicycle

miffy's dream
miffy at the zoo
miffy in hospital
miffy in the tent
miffy at the seaside
miffy in the snow
miffy goes flying
miffy at the playground
poppy pig
poppy pig is sick
boris on the mountain

boris in the snow
boris bear
boris and barbara
snuffy
snuffy's puppies
miffy's house
miffy at the gallery
aunt alice's party
grandpa and grandma bunn
poppy pig's garden
poppy pig's birthday

"het huis van nijntje"
Original text Dick Bruna 1991 © copyright Mercis Publishing BV.
Illustrations Dick Bruna © copyright Mercis BV 1991.
Published in Great Britain in 1998 by World International Ltd.,
Deanway Technology Centre, Wilmslow Road, Handforth, Cheshire SK9 3FB.
Original English translation © copyright Patricia Crampton 1997.
The moral right of the author has been asserted.
Publication licensed by Mercis Publishing BV, Amsterdam.
Printed by Sebald Sachsendruck Plauen, Germany. All rights reserved.
ISBN 0-7498-3594-X